Balloons in the Park

Where Does a Desire of a Little Boys' Dream to Make People Happy Lead Him to in Life?

MARY THERESA NELSON

Fulton Books, Inc.
Meadville, PA

Published by Fulton Books 2021

ISBN 978-1-64654-861-3 (paperback)
ISBN 978-1-64654-862-0 (digital)

Printed in the United States of America

In memory of my loving husband
Lt. Walter J. Nelson Jr.
To Kris, Pia and Mikael my daily
inspiration of love and family.

As Jack and his mom were walking through the park, the first scent of spring was in full bloom. The air was filled with daffodils, lilies, and the smell of fresh-cut green grass. Even the tall trees were showing their beautiful spring coat of leaves and swaying in the breeze.

The sounds of spring were filled with little children's laughter and chatter in so many different words of the world. Some children were playing in the sandboxes, building castles, and towns of make-believe with little babies in their doll carriages all under the watchful eye of Mom.

As Jack skipped through the park, he was invited by the smells of hot dogs, cotton candy, and pretzels from all the vendors. Each vendor displayed their wares in a different pushcart, and the sounds of the vendors working to prepare all these delights filled this area of the park.

As Jack walked along, he noticed an old man dressed like his grandpa. He shuffled along the park with the weight of a treasure of balloons in his hands. As the sun hit the balloons, the sky lit up in all shades of red, blue, green, and yellow. Suddenly, the little old man was surrounded by children filled with such delight.

As Mom and Jack walked through the park, Mom said to Jack, "What would you like to be when you grow up?"

Jack looked up at the sky and looked around the park and finally answered Mom, "I would like to sell balloons in the park."

Mom looked at Jack and said, "Why?"

Jack looked at Mom and replied, "Because selling balloons make kids happy, and I want to make kids happy."

Jack and Mom continued to walk through the park, looking at the children enjoying this wonderful spring day.

As they were leaving, Mom bought Jack a red balloon attached to a long red string. Jack thanked Mom and then said, "I think when I grow up, I will just walk around the park and give away balloons to all children."

Mom turned to Jack and asked, "Why?"

Jack said, "Mom, I want all children to have balloons. I want to help all of them, not just the ones with money."

Mom gave Jack a hug and replied, "Jack, I am so proud of you. That is very kind."

Mom and Jack went home to wait for Dad to come home from work. Dad worked for the New York City Fire Department in the emergency medical division. He rode in an ambulance and provided medical care to many people in the city of New York. Jack anxiously waited for Dad to return home from work because Dad always had a story about his day for Jack.

Dad came home from work and sat down at the table to eat dinner with Jack and Mom. Dad told Jack a story about a little girl who called 911 because her Barbie doll's leg fell off, and she was told at the nursery school to call 911 in case anyone gets hurt. Dad explained to Jack it was not a good idea to call 911 for Barbie, but Dad put Barbie's leg back for the little girl and even put a bandage on her leg. Dad told the little girl's Mom to please explain to the little girl that she does not need to call 911 to fix Barbie. Mom and Dad laughed about the Barbie story. Then Dad asked Mom and Jack what they did today.

Mom told Dad that they went to the park because it was a beautiful spring day.

Then Mom looked at Jack and said, "Jack, tell Dad what you want to do when you grow up."

Before Jack could answer, Mom gave Dad an encouraging look.

Jack said, "I want to sell balloons in the park or just give them to all the kids to make them happy."

Dad looked at Mom and then said, "That is great, Jack. You are very kind."

When Jack's little sister Mia was born, Jack took Dad to the park to buy Mia the biggest red balloon he could find on the day Mia and Mom came home from the hospital.

Jack went to elementary school, high school, and college. Throughout his high school and college days, Jack volunteer for many local church events, as well as doing work at the neighborhood volunteer ambulance organization.

For every special event, Jack was always given a balloon or would buy a balloon as a gift to someone special. Each graduation party, the house was filled with red, blue, purple, yellow, and green balloons. And as the guest left, the house Jack gave each child a balloon.

Jack always kept his dream to sell balloons or give balloons to children in his head as he grew into a man. Finally, Jack decided to become an emergency medical technician and work for the New York City Fire Department.

Many times, if he responded to a call where a child was hurt, he would make an animal balloon from a plastic glove to help the child to smile. Jack loved helping people, and his Mom and Dad were very proud of Jack that he chose to do this work.

At dinnertime, Jack and Dad would share stories of their day and the events in New York City. But in his heart, Jack always wanted to make children happy by giving them a balloon. He knew he was making people happy with his work as an EMT, but he kept this dream always in his heart. Many times, at dinner, Mom would recall the story of the day in the park when Jack said he would grow up to sell balloons in the park.

It was early November, and Jack came home from work so excited. As Dad was cooking and Mom and Mia were sharing their days, Jack told them something great happened today, and he will share it at dinner.

"Today the station got a call, there is work available at the Thanksgiving Day Parade."

Mom frowned because she hoped this holiday that they would be together as a family at Thanksgiving dinner.

Jack continued his story. "The assignment is to be a balloon handler at the Macy's Thanksgiving Day Parade. Since it is the 150th Anniversary of New York City's Fire Department, the department is looking for volunteers to handle Harold the Fireman." Jack was so excited and then said, "My dream to give balloons to children so they will be happy is finally coming true. As I handle that balloon and look at the smiling faces of all the children and adults at the parade, my dream will be fulfilled. So isn't that great?"

Mom and Dad smiled and said, "Yes, Jack, your dream has come true. That is great! We are so proud of you."

Thanksgiving Day was a cool crisp November day. Jack was very excited as he arrived at Central Park to finally live his dream. This dream to give children balloons to make them smile began in a small park in Brooklyn on a spring day and concluded in a large park on a cool crisp day in November as all of New York City was watching.

About the Author

Mary Theresa Nelson has been a devoted educator for over thirty years. Her first love has always been students in the early childhood grades and pre-kindergarten through second grade. Out of this love of working with young children, Mary Theresa always wanted to write a children's book. *Balloons in the Park* is a special story about a special little boy in her life. Mary Theresa lives in Brooklyn, New York, with her son, daughter, and grandson.